P9-CAN-674

The Humans of
ZIAX 11

by John Morressy

Illustrated by Stanley Skardinski

SCHOLASTIC BOOK SERVICES
New York Toronto London Auckland Sydney Tokyo

For the Little Guy

ISBN 0-590-30382-1

Text copyright © 1974 by John Morressy. Illustrations copyright ©
1974 by Stanley Skardinski. All rights reserved. This edition is
published by Scholastic Book Services, a division of Scholastic
Magazines, Inc., 50 West 44th Street, New York, N.Y. 10036, by
arrangement with Walker & Company.

12 11 10 9 8 7 6 5 4 3 2   9/7 0 1 2 3 4/8

Printed in the U. S. A.   11

Contents

PRISONER
OF THE
IMBUR

Toren awoke at the first light. All the pain was gone. He felt strong, and his head was clear. He knew that he was well again. This thought was so pleasant that for a time he could think of nothing else.

He got out of the low hammock and stood up slowly. For the fifth morning in a row, he did not feel dizzy. He raised his arms and stretched as tall as he could. There was no pain in his ribs or his arm. He was really well at last.

Very quietly, he went to the entrance of the hut. All was still in the village of the Imbur. He saw no one, and he heard nothing. Maybe this would be a good time to escape.

1

But it was foolish even to think of escape. A huge forest of gampal trees stood between him and Pioneer Base One, where the Earthmen lived. Toren could never find his way back alone. The hut had no door, and there were no guards. No one watched him, and yet he could not escape.

The Imbur called him their guest. They treated him well. All the same, he knew that he was a prisoner. A guest was free to come and go as he pleased, but Toren had to stay in his hut. The Imbur never spoke of taking him home. When he asked about going home, they told him it was not a good time for travelling. But they never explained why.

The Imbur were the natives of this planet that Earthmen had named Ziax II. They looked·different from humans, but they were not ugly or scary. They were about the same size as humans. They had six fingers on each hand. The sixth one served as a kind of extra thumb. Their faces were a lot like human faces, except that they had no nose. Their big round eyes made them look surprised all the time. Their heads, the backs of their hands, and their arms and legs were covered with a soft golden fur.

The Imbur dressed in a single loose garment that hung from their shoulders to their knees.

Toren had been given one of the Imbur garments. It felt good, but he missed his Pioneer clothing.

He went back to his hammock and lay down again. Now that he was well, he would have to make the Imbur take him home. But how could he make the Imbur do anything if they never listened to him?

He told himself that today, somehow, he would force them to listen. When he tried to think of a way of doing this, he could not. He thought and thought about it until he heard sounds from the other huts.

The Imbur were waking up. The village was coming to life. Soon Rilmat would arrive with some food. Toren felt a little better. Rilmat would help if he could.

HOW THE EARTHMEN CAME TO ZIAX 11

Rilmat was the only friend Toren had in the village. Toren guessed Rilmat was nice to him because they were about the same age.

Not that Toren understood the language of the Imbur. He could not speak even one word of it. Their talk sounded to him like a lot of chirps and whistles and humming noises. But somehow the Imbur had learned Toren's language. They spoke it well.

Whenever he had a visitor, Toren did most of the talking. At first, he spoke of nothing but Pioneer Base One. He missed his home and his parents and friends so much that he didn't want to talk about anything else. He didn't care whether anyone listened or not.

But Rilmat listened. He must have had trouble understanding things, because he was always asking questions. He didn't know even the simplest things about the way Earthmen lived.

When Toren tried to explain how he had got hurt, he had to speak of the skimmers. That was what the Earth Pioneers called the skysleds in which they travelled just above the treetops.

Toren told how he had gone on a map-making flight with his father. They were crossing the great gampal forest that covered half the planet. Then the skimmer had gone out of control, and Toren had been thrown out of it.

Rilmat listened very politely. Then he said, "This is a joke, is it not? Nothing can travel in the air."

Toren had to explain that the Earthmen really could fly. After all, if they could come to Ziax II from another world, surely they could fly forty feet off the ground!

But once Toren spoke of Earth, he had to explain what Earth was. It took a long time for Rilmat to understand that there were other worlds with people on them. And then Rilmat asked Toren why the Earthmen had left their own world and come to Ziax II.

Toren was not too sure about that himself. He had not been born when the mother ship left Earth. The grown-ups sometimes spoke of "pollution," but Toren was not sure what this word meant. He only knew that when a world became polluted, the people had to leave and seek a new one. That was what the Pioneers had done.

Once he had settled the question of Earth, Toren was able to explain about the skimmers.

Rilmat's people had nothing like them. In fact, there were no birds or flying insects anywhere on Ziax II. Rilmat had never seen anything fly, and he could not think of such a thing.

When Toren finally convinced him that skimmers really did exist, Rilmat had another question. "Why do your people use these machines and not walk?" he asked.

"The skimmers are faster than walking," Toren told him.

"Is it good to go fast?"

"Yes. Well, I guess it is. I never thought about it before," Toren said.

Rilmat was not happy. He asked, "Why is it good? From your skimmers you can see nothing in the forest below. You have told me so. Is it better to be fast or to see the things around you?"

After that, Toren did not talk about the skimmers.

On another day, he told about the atmosphere dome and the food-making machine at the base. When he was finished, Toren felt very pleased. Even Rilmat was sure to see how great the atmosphere dome was.

Then came the questions.

"But, if the air is not bad on Ziax II, why do you shut it out?" Rilmat asked.

"To make it safer, I guess," Toren said.

"Is the air of my world bad?"

"No, it's fine, Rilmat. It's very good."

"Then why do the Earthmen hide from it?" Rilmat asked.

Toren could not answer that, either. He changed the subject to the food-making machine. Rilmat had another question.

"The fruit of the gampal tree is everywhere. So why do the Earth Pioneers eat food made by a machine?" he asked.

Again, Toren had no answer. After that, he let Rilmat do most of the talking.

RILMAT

Rilmat came in and sat down beside the hammock. He brought a platter of fruits for Toren's breakfast.

"Fresh gampal fruit, Toren. I gathered it myself on my way here," he said.

"Thanks, Rilmat. I'm hungry this morning." Toren took one of the bright golden fruits and bit into it.

"Do you feel better?" Rilmat asked.

Toren could not answer with his mouth full of the sweet food. He nodded his head. Rilmat just looked at him. The Imbur could not move their heads as the Earthmen did. Nods and head-shaking meant nothing to them.

9

Toren gulped down the fruit and said, "Yes, I do. I feel well enough to start for home."

"The forest is dangerous," his friend said.

"I don't care. I want to go home. Will you help me, Rilmat?"

"I will help you. What shall I do?" Rilmat asked.

"Help me find my way through the forest," Toren said.

Rilmat thought about that for a time. Then he

said, "I don't have the power to tell you what to do, Toren. I must bring the Watchers."

The Watchers were leaders among the Imbur. They were the ones who had told Toren that it was not the right time to go into the forest. But maybe with Rilmat's help he could change their minds.

Toren was about to tell Rilmat to go for the Watchers when he heard footsteps. Rilmat heard them, too. He looked out the doorway. Then he said to Toren, "The Watchers are coming."

Toren's heart beat faster. It was hard not to be afraid. He told himself once more that Earth Pioneers feared nothing. They did not let themselves become prisoners. Earthmen told people what they wanted done, and people did it. That was always the way.

Earth Pioneers had won over a thousand worlds more dangerous than Ziax II. Someday they would rule over the whole galaxy. No true Pioneer would be scared by aliens like the Imbur. They looked too soft and furry.

And yet Toren was afraid. No one knew what happened to Earthmen who strayed from the base. Six Earthmen had been lost in the great gampal forest before Toren. None had returned, and no trace of them was ever found.

Maybe they had starved. Maybe they had been

eaten by wild beasts. Or they might have been captured by the Imbur. And if that were so, then what had become of them?

Toren would know very soon.

THE WATCHERS

The Watchers came into the hut. They were taller than Toren and Rilmat. But they were not as tall as Toren's father. Toren wished his father were with him now. There would be nothing to fear then. But his father was far away at the base. Toren was alone. He had to be brave all by himself.

The Watchers bowed from the waist. Then they put their hands, palms outward, to their foreheads. This was the Imbur way of saying hello. Toren returned the gesture.

"We see that you are well. This makes us glad," one of them said in his deep voice.

The Imbur always had to tell him whether they

were happy or sad. The look on their faces never changed. At first Toren had had trouble understanding their feelings. But now he could tell from the way they sounded.

"I'm well and I want to go home," he said.

The Watcher acted as if he had not heard Toren's words. He held out his hands and said, "We have this for you."

Toren took the bundle from him and opened it. He was happy to find his Pioneer suit, boots, and helmet. He thought that they had been stolen by the Imbur, or else lost in the forest.

"They have been made clean. The places where they were torn have been mended," the Watcher said.

Toren looked his things over carefully. He was amazed. The suit was spotless. The boots shone. The helmet looked like new. His things looked as good as when they had come from the machine at Pioneer Base One. In fact, they looked a little better.

He could not understand how the Imbur had done such a thing. They had no machines like the Earthmen.

"Thank you very much," he said.

"Is it your wish to wear your own clothes?" the Watcher asked.

"It's my wish to go home," Toren said.

"Only the Ru-Imbur can say when it is time to enter the forest," said the Watcher.

"Then I want to speak to the Ru-Imbur!" Toren cried.

The Watchers turned to face one another. They spoke in their own language. Then they turned to Toren and said, "You may come with us to the Ru-Imbur."

"Will he take me home?" Toren asked.

"He will do what is wise. Come," said the Watcher.

Toren was excited. He forgot his fear and started to run out of the hut. Rilmat had to remind him to change into his Pioneer clothing.

THE
RU=IMBUR

Toren walked between the two Imbur. They went down a long street to a large hut at the very end. The street was lined with huts. They were woven from living plants. Thick gampal trees rose over the huts and hid them from view. Anyone overhead in a skimmer would not be able to see them.

They finally came to the hut. An Imbur in a bright garment of many stripes rose to give the greeting. Toren returned it. Then he folded his arms as his father always did in meetings at the base. He stood facing the Imbur. He felt braver now. He was sure he could make them listen to him.

"I am the Ru-Imbur, leader of the forest people," said the figure in the striped garment. He sounded friendly. "Does our guest wish to tell us how he is known to his people?"

Toren guessed that this was the Imbur way of asking his name. No one in the village had ever come right out and asked his name before. The Imbur were too polite to do such a thing. Only Rilmat knew his name because Toren had told him.

"I'm Toren Mallixxan, son of Garet Mallixxan. He is the head of the Earth force at Pioneer Base One on planet Ziax II," Toren said.

The Ru-Imbur spoke his own language to those on either side of him. Then he asked Toren, "Is our guest truly the son of a leader among the Earth people?"

"Yes, I am. And my father will soon come to find me. He will bring me back home," Toren replied.

The Imbur seemed excited by these words. Toren was glad he had been brave. The Imbur had not scared him into keeping silent. It was clear that the idea of his father coming soon scared them. They would surely let him go now.

The Ru-Imbur seemed to be the most upset of all. He moved around the hut and talked to

18

everyone. He spoke longest with Rilmat. Then he turned to Toren.

"This is a brave thing your father does, but it is very dangerous," he said in a worried voice.

Toren thought they were trying to trick him because he was so young. But he was not fooled. Earth Pioneers had nothing to fear from these creatures. He had not seen a single weapon in the entire village. There was no danger here.

"My father is not afraid of you or of anyone else. He'll find me," Toren said.

"But this is the breeding time of the sork! The forests are full of danger. The sork will kill anything to feed their young. Do your people know about them, Toren Mallixxan?" the Ru-Imbur asked.

Toren felt stupid. Perhaps they had been telling the truth all along. "We...we know there are dangerous beasts in the forest. But we didn't know...We never thought..." His voice became weaker.

"It is a serious matter. We would have brought you to your own people to get well if the way had been clear. But we have been waiting for the sork to move on to their hunting grounds."

"Pioneers can take care of a sork," Toren said boldly.

The Ru-Imbur said, "No creature can stand against the sork, Toren Mallixxan. Not even the Earth Pioneers can do that. We have found some of your people dead in the forest. They had weapons, but the sork killed them." The Ru-Imbur was silent for a time. He was thinking very deeply about something important. The others said nothing. They all waited for him to speak. At last he said, "We will enter the forest."

One of the other Imbur stood. He said, "In a short time, the sork will be gone. Can we not wait until that time?"

The Ru-Imbur replied, "No, we cannot. The father and friends of our guest are in danger. We must save them. Come, let us get ready."

THE GAMPAL FOREST

The Imbur moved quickly. Within a few minutes, the entire village was hard at work getting ready for the trip. At noon, a party of thirty-one Imbur and Toren left to save the Earth Pioneers from the sork.

Rilmat came with them. He and Toren walked side by side. They saw no other creatures in the forest on the first day. Rilmat told Toren that this was a sign the sork were near. Every living thing fled from the sork.

The news made Toren very uneasy. Here they were, walking into the forest where sork might appear at any moment. And no one had a weapon!

22

The Imbur didn't even seem the least bit worried. Yet they all knew how dangerous the sork were.

"If sork are so dangerous, why are we going through the forest unarmed?" Toren asked his friend.

Rilmat stared at him for a moment. Then he made a high whistling sound. This was the Imbur sound for laughter. He held out his arms. "Again, you make a joke, Toren. We have our arms," he said, and went on laughing.

"No, no, that's not what I mean," Toren said. "I'm not joking. I'm worried. We have no weapons. We can't defend ourselves."

"Imbur use no weapons. The Ru-Imbur will protect us."

"But he has no weapons, either! Aren't the sork dangerous? How can you kill them without weapons?" Toren asked.

Rilmat stopped in his tracks. He looked at Toren as if he had said something terrible. He started to speak. But then, without a word, he turned and walked away. Toren was about to follow him, but at that moment the lead scout called a halt to make camp for the night. There was work to be done at once.

The Imbur quickly wove a fence from the vines of the gampal trees around them. Toren saw that

they did not cut the vines from the trees. They worked with the living plants, weaving them into a tight fence. Once this was done, each of the Imbur laid his sleeping mat down in some cozy place. Many of them went to sleep at once, even though it was not yet dark. Toren saw no guards. But then one of the Imbur told him that sork do not hunt by night.

Toren ate. Then he threw himself down on his mat. He looked up at the stars that hung above Ziax II. He thought about his stay with the Imbur. He no longer feared them or thought they wanted to harm him. In a funny way, he had come to like them. But he still could not always understand them. Rilmat seemed angry and hurt. Toren could not figure out why. It puzzled him.

The Imbur were backward in so many ways. They lived under the open sky. Here in the camp, you could feel the breezes and hear all the night sounds. You could smell the forest smells. How different it was from Pioneer Base One, with its dome overhead and the soft purr of its machines! Sometimes, out here, it rained and you got wet. That never happened under the dome. There, everything was always the same.

And yet, somehow, the Imbur seemed happy. Toren could not understand why they were happy living in such a way. But he could see that they were. In fact, sometimes they seemed a lot happier than the people at the base.

That made no sense at all to Toren. The Earth Pioneers had everything. The poor Imbur had nothing. As he drifted off to sleep, Toren thought of their happiness. How could it be?

THE
SORK

Things happened fast the next day. Toren was not sure what was going on until it was all over.

He was walking alone. Rilmat still had not spoken to him. By this time, Toren was angry with his friend. He had made up his mind not to speak first. If Rilmat wanted to be mad for some stupid reason, let him. He could get along without Rilmat.

Suddenly, up ahead, the Imbur were crying out. They sounded excited and scared. Then Toren heard a scream and a roar that seemed to shake the trees. He looked up. There before him was something so big and awful that he felt his knees shake.

27

It looked like all the monsters of the galaxy rolled into one. No one had to tell him what it was. Toren knew he was looking at a sork.

It had a big head. Its mouth was filled with long teeth that dripped as it turned from side to side. Its eyes were long and narrow and very bright. When it reared up and slashed out with its forepaws, it was almost as tall as the treetops. The sork seemed to be covered with spines. It had more teeth and claws than anything Toren had ever dreamed of. It gave off loud roars that made his bones shake.

All at once the rest of the Imbur were gone. The Ru-Imbur stood alone in front of the sork. He showed no fear. He raised his hands and began to chant sounds. Toren had not heard them before. All around him, the voices of the Imbur rose and joined in the chant.

The sork came forward a few paces. Then it stopped. It seemed confused. The chant grew louder. The creature sank to its belly. It crawled closer to the Ru-Imbur. Then it growled once, loudly. The sork lashed out with its forepaw. It missed the Ru-Imbur by no more than a hand's length. The leader of the forest people did not move or pause in his chant. He went right on as if nothing had happened. The sork shuddered once. It gave a sound like a sigh, and then lay still.

Imbur began to step from behind the trees. The Ru-Imbur covered his face for a time, as if he were very tired. Some of the others went to him, and he leaned on them until his strength returned. Then he ordered the Imbur to move on.

"Is the sork dead?" Toren asked a passing Imbur.

"Of course not. It will stay in the long sleep until we are safely away," the Imbur said.

"What's the long sleep? When will you kill it?" Toren called after him. But he got no answer. He decided to ask the Ru-Imbur himself.

The leader was standing by the fallen sork. He was looking down on the great beast as if he felt sorry for it. Toren asked, "Aren't you going to kill it?"

"No," was the answer.

"Why not? If you don't kill the sork, it might wake up and kill us!" Toren said, amazed at this reply.

"That does not make it right to kill. The sork is an unknowing one. Its nature is to kill. That is not our nature," the Ru-Imbur said. His voice was tired and very gentle. But Toren felt he was being told something important.

"Sometimes you have to kill," Toren said. He

30

tried to sound firm and sure of himself. But he was no longer sure of what he said.

"No, Toren. We have a law. It forbids us to take the life of another being."

Toren heard that with surprise. "My people have a law like that, too," he said.

The Ru-Imbur was silent for a time. Then he turned and spoke to other Imbur. They all turned to Toren. Their leader asked, "Do the Earth Pioneers truly have the same law?"

"Yes. It's an old law on Earth," Toren said.

The Imbur talked among themselves. They seemed excited. One of them asked, "How can that be? You say Earthmen have the law, and yet they take life. That does not make sense!"

Toren found that he could not explain. He said what he had said before. "Sometimes you have to." But it sounded no better now than it had then. He began to feel very stupid and ashamed. And yet he had done or said nothing wrong.

The Ru-Imbur leaned down and touched him on the shoulders. In a kind voice, he said, "Only the unknowing can say that, Toren. You have been with the Imbur. You know the truth now."

These words, and the touch of the Ru-Imbur, made Toren feel something inside. He could not explain what was happening. It was as if someone were helping him to dream a dream. The dream was his own, but others were joining in it. They were helping him to dream it right.

He understood why Rilmat had been so angry when he spoke of weapons and killing. The Imbur did not believe in such things. They could not understand the Earthmen. The Earthmen were like them and yet they were not. Toren felt for a moment that the Imbur's way of life made sense. Then the Ru-Imbur removed his hand. At once the feeling was gone.

The first thing Toren did that night was to ask Rilmat to forgive him. Rilmat did.

THE EARTHMEN AND THE SORK

Toren woke up all at once the next morning. He felt nervous and uneasy. He sat up and looked around. All the Imbur were still sleeping. He heard nothing but the soft sound of the gampal trees. Everything was asleep and yet he felt danger was near.

He tried to go back to sleep, but he could not. He turned to Rilmat. His friend was awake.

As soon as he saw Toren, Rilmat asked, "Do you feel it, too?"

"Yes. Something's wrong. But I don't understand."

It was getting light. Rilmat stood up and looked around. He said, "We must wake my father."

Rilmat had never spoken of his father before. Toren wondered which of the Imbur it could be. He was about to ask when a roar split the air. A sork reared up outside the fence of woven vines. It began to claw its way through. The Imbur sprang up all around. Another roar came from the far side of the camp. Then came more roars from all sides. The sork were everywhere.

Toren ran to where the Ru-Imbur stood with a little group of Watchers. The sork were tearing through the vine fence. Their roaring made his bones shake. But once the Imbur began their chant, he felt no fear.

All at once, he found himself joining in the chant. The strange sounds came from his lips easily. He was surprised to find himself doing this. But at the same time, it felt right. It was like something he had done many times before. He knew exactly what to do.

One of the sork burst through the vine fence. But once it was inside the camp, its growling grew less. The Imbur chanted louder and louder. The creature fell to the ground. Other sork came. But they too were dazed by the chant.

Then, from the forest nearby, came the sharp snapping of Pioneer handguns. The fallen sork grew alert again. It lifted its head and gave an awful roar. It began to climb to its feet.

34

Part of the fence went up in a ball of flame. Toren saw men in Pioneer suits running through the opening. They fired on the sork as they ran. The huge creatures turned from the Imbur and began to attack the Earthmen.

"It's my father! He's come to help us!" Toren cried.

The Ru-Imbur turned to him. "No, Toren! You must make him stop shooting. We might all be destroyed!"

The Earthmen all fired on one sork. It fell back and landed on the ground. But the other sork kept closing in.

"They're winning! They'll get rid of the sork. Then Ziax II will be safe!" Toren said.

Again the Ru-Imbur placed his hands on Toren's shoulders. The noise around them became distant. Toren could hear the Ru-Imbur's words clearly. "You know the truth now, Toren. Killing makes nothing safe. Even the sork have the right to live."

Everything was clear. Toren looked up into the Ru-Imbur's round eyes. "Yes. Now I understand," he said.

The Ru-Imbur lifted his hands. At once, Toren heard again the noise all around them. He broke away from the Imbur. He ran toward the

Earthmen, waving his arms. The smoke and dust were so thick that he could hardly see them.

"Stop shooting!" he shouted. "Don't shoot anymore!"

But they could not hear him. He had to get closer. As he ran, a sork turned its cold eyes on him. Toren stopped in his tracks. He stood still. The sork looked at the Earthmen, then at Toren. It seemed to be thinking about whom to attack. When it turned to the Earthmen, Toren knew that he must help them.

He picked up a gampal fruit lying near his feet. He flung it at the sork. When the sork turned on him, Toren began to chant. The beast moved closer. But Toren stood firm.

The sork slowed, but it still kept coming. Its steps shook the ground. Its roars sent shivers down Toren's spine. Toren felt himself becoming weaker and weaker. It seemed as if all his strength were going into the chant. But he did not move. He had to give the Earthmen time to escape.

The sork reared up before him and raised its claws. Toren heard the chant of the Imbur loud behind him. Then everything went black.

THE RU-IMBUR EXPLAINS

When Toren woke, Rilmat and the Ru-Imbur were on either side of him. He blinked and sat up. A sork lay at his feet.

The Ru-Imbur said, "You did well. The sork-chant takes much strength."

"But how did I know it? I'm not an Imbur, I'm an Earthman!"

The Ru-Imbur and Rilmat looked at one another. Then the Ru-Imbur said, "The time has come to explain. When my son found you in the forest..."

"Rilmat? Is Rilmat your son?" Toren burst in.

"Yes, Toren," his friend said. "When I found

38

you in the forest, you were badly hurt. We could not take you to your own people for healing. We had to heal you ourselves. My father and I gave you our own blood to make you well. Now, wherever you go, part of us will always be part of you."

"Then I *am* an Imbur," Toren said.

The Ru-Imbur helped him to his feet. "Imbur, Earthmen, all are one, Toren. Each of us has his special gifts. The Earthmen are very brave. They can make wonderful machines. The Imbur can speak the languages of all beings. And you will be able to do the things of both people."

The news caused a strange feeling in Toren. Now, when his return to Pioneer Base One was so close, he did not want to leave the Imbur. It seemed that only now, when they were parting, he really understood them. In a way, Rilmat and the Ru-Imbur were his own people, as much as the Earthmen.

"Must I leave the Imbur now?" Toren asked.

"Yes, you must. You are the Earth Pioneers' last hope."

"Me? Their last hope? What do you mean?" Toren asked. The Ru-Imbur had to be joking.

"Yes, Toren. Earthmen fear what they do not know and cannot understand. Sometimes their fear makes them cruel," Rilmat said.

"Like when they tried to kill the sork?"

"Yes," said the Ru-Imbur. "You must change this."

"But how can I?" Toren asked. He felt helpless.

The Ru-Imbur put a hand on Toren's shoulder. Rilmat laid his hand on Toren's other shoulder. Then he said, "We will be with you when you need us. Only you will know."

The Ru-Imbur said, "We have made you one of the knowing ones. Now you must teach the Earthmen...to be truly human!"

"I will. I promise you, I will," Toren said.

"Now, if your strength is back, we will start. The Earthmen cannot be far away," said the Ru-Imbur.

Four sork lay sleeping in the camp-site. That was far fewer than the number that had attacked. Toren wondered how far off the others were.

Suddenly, from the distant forest, there came the sound of roars and shooting. It was clear now where the sork had gone.

COMMANDER
MALLIXXAN

Toren and the Imbur raced through the gampal forest. They ran toward the sound of shooting. Before they reached the place, the shooting stopped. The roars grew louder. Toren feared that the sork had defeated the Pioneers. He urged the Imbur on.

At last they reached the Pioneers. The Earthmen were on a high ledge. A smooth cliff rose behind them. They were out of the sork's reach, but there was no way to escape. Toren saw his father. He held a weapon in each hand. Some of the Earthmen seemed to be hurt.

The Ru-Imbur came to Toren. "We will make

42

the sork sleep," he said. "But first, the Earthmen must be warned not to use their weapons."

Toren looked at the sork waiting hungrily by the foot of the cliff. There were about a dozen of them. He swallowed hard. "I'll tell them," he said.

He took a few steps. Then he turned to Rilmat and the Ru-Imbur. "Will you come back to the base with us when it's all over?" he asked.

The Ru-Imbur came to Toren. He touched his forehead. "We will always be with you now," he said.

Toren understood. He felt as if he were growing stronger. He turned and started toward the sork.

Whether it was fear or the help of the Imbur, Toren did not know. But, somehow, he managed to race past the sork before they knew he was there. He jumped over a fallen gampal tree and sprang to the lower rocks. A sork growled behind him. Someone from above called his name.

"Hold your fire! Don't shoot!" he cried.

He scrambled up the rocks. The sork came closer, and Toren heard its claws scrape on the rock just below his feet. Then strong hands pulled him to the ledge.

"It's Toren! He's alive!" the men shouted.

His father, Commander Mallixxan, greeted

him. Toren forgot all his fear and threw his arms around the tall, strong man who lifted him high in the air.

"Toren, you look better than ever! We never expected to find you alive!" his father shouted.

"The Imbur saved me," Toren said.

"Those furry creatures? The forest dwellers?"

"Yes. And now they're going to save us all," Toren said.

Toren's father looked down on him. A few of the men laughed. Commander Mallixxan said, "You really mean that, don't you, son?"

"Yes, I do. They'll put the sork to sleep, and then we can return safely to the base."

One of the men said, "Good. When they're asleep, we can wipe those monsters out once and for all."

"No. You must agree to hold your fire," Toren said firmly.

"Those things are killers!" the man cried.

"They don't know any better. We do. Will you promise not to fire?" Toren asked them.

Commander Mallixxan put away his guns. He turned to the others. "We'll hold our fire," he said.

"But, Commander — " the man started to say.

"That's an order. Our weapons haven't done us much good. Maybe the forest people have a better way," Commander Mallixxan said. He turned to his son. "All right, Toren. We won't fire anymore."

Toren was proud of his father. He stepped to the front of the ledge. He waved toward the forest, where the Imbur were hidden. Their chant began to rise. One by one, the sork became still. Commander Mallixxan was amazed.

"I *thought* that's what they did back at the clearing. But I didn't believe my eyes and ears! It really works, Toren!" he exclaimed.

When the last sork had fallen, the chanting stopped. The Ru-Imbur stepped from the gampal forest so all could see him. He raised his hands to his forehead. Toren returned the gesture.

Once long ago, it seemed, when he first saw an Imbur, Toren had smiled. He thought then that they were an odd-looking kind of creature. They appeared small and weak to him. But now the Ru-Imbur looked proud and fine. Toren was sad to see him turn and disappear into the forest. Still, he was happy to have lived among the forest people, even for a short time. He remembered the Ru-Imbur's words: "Imbur, Earthmen, all are one." All were human. They could share this planet in peace. He would help to bring it about.

When the Ru-Imbur was gone, Toren's father

asked about the farewell gesture he and Toren had made. Toren explained it.

"That's a good thing to know," his father said. "You'll have to teach it to the Pioneers."

Toren felt the wisdom of the Imbur stirring in his mind. It was like a bright light in the evening shadows. "I'll teach you everything I learned from them, Father," he said. "But first, let's go home."

The Drought on
ZIAX II

by John Morressy

Illustrated by Stanley Skardinski

SCHOLASTIC BOOK SERVICES
New York Toronto London Auckland Sydney Tokyo

ISBN 0-590-30382-1

Text copyright © 1978 by John Morressy. Illustrations copyright © 1978 by Stanley Skardinski. All rights reserved. This edition is published by Scholastic Book Services, a division of Scholastic Magazines, Inc., 50 West 44th Street, New York, N. Y. 10036, by arrangement with Walker & Company.

12 11 10 9 8 7 6 5 4 3 2   9/7 0 1 2 3 4/8

Printed in the U. S. A.   11

CONTENTS

THE SEARCHERS

Toren Mallixxan rested in the shade of a gampal tree, talking to his friends. The long summer of Ziax II was nearly over, but the days were still hot. The heat and the talking had made Toren very thirsty. He reached for his canteen, but then he remembered his father's orders. Water was strictly rationed. So he licked his dry lips and thought of the cool waters of Earth.

For someone born in space, Toren knew a great deal about Earth. He read all the material in the Base Library. He studied the maps and globes in the schoolroom at Pioneer Base One. Whenever

1

the older Pioneers spoke of their home world, Earth, Toren listened closely to all they said.

The friends who sat with Toren were not humans from the Pioneer Base. They were Imbur, the forest people of Ziax II.

The Imbur had round eyes, and no noses, and six fingers on each hand, but otherwise they looked much like the people from Earth. Their bare arms and legs, and their heads, were covered with soft golden fur. They were shy and gentle people who lived at peace on their world.

The Imbur dressed differently from the Pioneers. Toren and the other Pioneers wore silver suits and boots, but the Imbur each wore a single loose garment that reached from the shoulders to the knees. Stripes on the garment showed the age and rank of the Imbur who wore it.

Toren spoke to them of the land and water of the Earth. The Imbur all spoke the Earthmen's language, but they did not always understand every word. When Toren spoke of the oceans, rivers, and lakes, the Imbur had many questions. He tried to explain.

"An ocean is a huge body of water," he said.

"How can water be a body?" one Imbur asked.

"Well, I don't mean like an Imbur body, or a Pioneer's body. Not *that* kind of body."

"What kind of body, then?" another Imbur asked.

Toren scratched his head and thought for a time. The Imbur were always asking questions like that one. They seemed like very simple questions, but when he tried to answer them, he found that they were not simple at all. Still, he had to try. He did not want them thinking that Earth people were stupid.

"An ocean is so much water that if you were out in the middle of it, you couldn't see anything but water wherever you looked," he explained. "A lake is smaller than an ocean, but still very big."

No one said anything for a moment, then someone asked, "How can humans live in all that water?"

"We live on the land. Fish live in the water," Toren said.

"What is fish?" several Imbur asked at once.

Toren sighed. "Fish are creatures made to live in water. Humans are made to live on the land." He patted the firm ground beside him. "Like this, you know. Land. Solid ground."

The Imbur looked at each other. Toren wondered if they understood. It was hard to tell what an Imbur was thinking, because the expression on an Imbur's face never changed. With their big

round eyes, the Imbur always looked surprised.

"Things that live in the water must be very small," said Rilmat. He was Toren's best friend among the Imbur.

"Some of them are bigger than a sork," Toren said.

The Imbur did not change expression, but they made a high clicking sound that showed their surprise. The sork were the biggest creatures living on Ziax II. They were ferocious and very dangerous. Anything bigger than a sork would be frightening to see.

"How can anything so big live in a tiny trickle of water?" Rilmat asked.

At once, Toren understood why they were confused. They simply could not imagine a large body of water, like an ocean or a lake. Again, he tried to explain.

"Try to think of water that reaches as far in all directions as the gampal forest," he said. "Big creatures could live in that couldn't they?"

"Where would so much water come from?" one of the Imbur asked.

"Water comes bubbling up from the ground in little puddles," said another.

"Or it trickles down from the rocks," said a third.

"It's not like that on Earth," Toren said. "Earth is different. On the surface of Earth, there's three times as much water as land."

They all looked at him and licked their dry lips. "Then Earth is a very fortunate world," Rilmat said. The rest agreed.

Toren climbed to his feet. He was hot and very thirsty, but they had important work ahead. He held out his hand to help Rilmat.

"Ziax II is a good world, too, Rilmat," he said. "We'll find water soon. If it's out there, we'll find it."

The others moved away to rejoin their search teams. Very softly, so no one could hear, Rilmat said, "Suppose there is no water out there, Toren?"

THE
THIRSTING
WORLD

The fact is, all the inhabitants of Ziax II were in trouble. The Earth Pioneers had noticed it first.

During the long summer, the water supply began to fail. By midsummer, the Pioneers' crops were dying. No one knew why.

A solution had to be found quickly. If the Pioneers' crop failed, the Earthmen could still survive by eating the fruit of the gampal tree. That was how the Imbur lived. But the trees were withering, too. If the crops failed and the trees died, everyone on the planet might starve.

Commander Mallixxan, leader of the Earth Pioneers, declared an emergency. He issued strict rules for using the water on hand. He arranged to

meet with the leader of the Imbur, hoping that by working together, the Imbur and the Pioneers could solve their problem.

The leader of the Imbur was called the Ru-Imbur. He and the Earthmen's leader knew one another through their sons. Toren, the Commander's son, was a close friend of Rilmat, the son of the Ru-Imbur.

Commander Mallixxan and the Ru-Imbur met for a long time. The next day, the leaders of both races gathered at the base. The Watchers, wisest of the Imbur, explained the water sources in the gampal forest. The Pioneer Council showed how the Earthmen obtained and purified water from their wells. They were able to learn much from each other. But after all the meetings, they still had no solution.

The water level fell lower each day. Crops turned yellow, and then brown. The plants withered. In the forest, the gampal trees sagged and wilted. And still no one knew why.

One thing was decided. If the deep wells at Pioneer Base One could not supply water, then new sources had to be found at once. The Pioneers and the Imbur agreed to form teams to search the forest for water.

The search had to be made on foot. The low-

flying skysleds used by the Pioneers moved too fast. An observer in a skimmer, as the skysleds were called, could miss many details of the ground beneath him. Every day, skimmers were used to bring supplies and replacements for the search teams. But the work was slow, and hot, and disappointing.

They had been searching for ten days, so far. They had found nothing. And the water supply kept sinking lower.

THE DESTRUCTION OF THE SORK

Late in the day, the Earthmen and the Imbur separated to make camp. The Earth Pioneers pitched tents for the night. The Imbur wove a high enclosure from the living vines of the gampal tree, and slept inside it.

Toren had lived with the Imbur for a time. He liked to sleep as they did, in the open, under the stars. But the Pioneers preferred their tents. The Imbur could not understand how anyone could sleep like this. The Earthmen cut themselves off from the sky and the stars and the cool night breeze. So the two races lived in separate encampments.

Toren saw his father standing alone by the entrance to his tent. The search team leaders had just reported to him. No one had found water. His father looked worried. Toren tried to cheer him up.

"Don't worry, Father. We'll find water soon," he said.

His father sighed. "That's not my only worry, Toren."

"What's the matter? Can I help?" Toren asked.

His father did not answer at once, then he said, "Maybe you can. Come on inside."

They went into the command tent. Commander Mallixxan closed the tent flap behind them, so no one would enter. He and Toren sat in folding chairs.

"I spoke with the Ru-Imbur today, Toren. He's displeased because we've been shooting the sork," Commander Mallixxan said. "I can't seem to make him understand how dangerous sork are to us."

The sork were not only dangerous creatures, they were fearful to look upon. A full-grown sork was more than twice as tall as a man. It had a gaping mouth full of long teeth. Big bulging eyes with slitted pupils glared from its forehead. It could snap the trunk of a gampal tree in its claws. Sork had killed and injured many Pioneers in the

12

early days of settlement on Ziax II. To protect themselves, the Pioneers had taken to shooting all sork on sight.

The Imbur believed that this was wrong. Imbur had a way of controlling the sork without using weapons. By chanting certain sounds, they could put the creatures into a deep sleep. They tried to teach the Earthmen their chant. But the Earthmen did not trust this method. They felt safer using their weapons. Imbur did not believe in taking life, and so the use of weapons on the sork troubled them.

"The chant of the Imbur *will* stop the sork, Father. You've seen that for yourself," Toren said.

"Yes, I have. But the men claim that they can't make the chant work as well as the Imbur can. The sounds just don't come naturally to a human throat."

"It isn't easy, Father. But they could learn. I learned it, didn't I?"

"True, you did," Commander Mallixxan admitted. "But you lived among the Imbur. Until the men learn it, they have to protect themselves. I respect the beliefs of the Imbur, son. I don't want them to think of us as savages. But if I must choose between the lives of my people and the lives of sork, then I'll wipe out every sork on Ziax II, if I must."

"Maybe we've already done that," Toren said.

"What do you mean?" his father quickly asked.

"Well, we've been in the forest ten days, and no one has seen a sork. And they haven't been sighted around the base all summer."

Commander Mallixxan frowned. "You're right, Toren. I hadn't thought of that. What about the Imbur? Have they seen any?"

"No. I asked Rilmat yesterday. He said none of the Imbur have seen a sork for a long time," Toren said.

"I guess that explains why the Ru-Imbur is unhappy. He thinks we've killed all the sork. And maybe we have." Commander Mallixxan laid a hand on his son's shoulder. "Do you still want to help me?" he asked.

"Yes, I do," Toren replied.

"All right, then. Tomorrow, when we split into teams, you go with the Ru-Imbur's group. Talk to him. Let him know how the Pioneers feel. Maybe if he realizes that they're simply acting out of fear, he'll be more understanding. Will you do that for me, son?" Commander Mallixxan asked.

Toren agreed to help in any way he could.

UNKNOWING
ONES

The next day Toren was part of a search team that included the Ru-Imbur, Rilmat, and two Pioneers. As they moved off to their designated search area, Toren stayed close to the Ru-Imbur. He was waiting for the chance to talk to him apart from the others.

After a time the Pioneers separated from the others. Toren saw his opportunity to speak.

"My father says that you're displeased because some of the Pioneers have killed sork," he said.

"You know that the Imbur never take life, Toren," the Ru-Imbur replied.

"But you can use the chant. It works for you. It doesn't work for the Pioneers."

"It would work, if they tried harder."

"But that would take time. What would they do in the meantime for protection?" Toren asked.

"We would help to keep the sork away. But the Pioneers do not ask for our help. They use their weapons instead," the Ru-Imbur said.

"Maybe they just don't trust the chant," Toren said. Quickly, he added, "I do, because I've seen it work. And I've used it myself. But to a Pioneer, it's different. They've learned to trust their weapons."

The Ru-Imbur's voice sounded sad as he spoke. "That is the great problem, Toren. The Pioneers trust only their weapons. Your people may have destroyed the last sork on Ziax II."

Toren felt that the Ru-Imbur did not really understand. He seemed to think that sork were as important as people. Toren said, "What if we have? We saved lives. What good is a sork, anyway? It's just a big ugly thing that destroys everything it sees."

"The sork knows no better. The Earthmen do. To kill the last of any creature is a terrible deed, Toren, whatever the reason."

They walked on for a time without speaking. Toren began to feel ashamed of what he had said. Finally, he asked, "You don't like Earthmen very much, do you?"

The Ru-Imbar halted, stooped down, and placed his hands on Toren's shoulders. This was a special way of communicating that the Imbur sometimes used. Toren had learned it, and other Imbur ways, when he lived among them.

"Toren, you are as close to me as Rilmat is. I admire your father and mother and all the Earth Pioneers. But it troubles me that even though they hate and fear the sork, the Pioneers act like sork themselves. The sork kills because it is an unknowing one. It cannot help but kill. But the Earthmen have intelligence, and yet they, too, kill," the Ru-Imbur said.

Deep inside Toren's mind, the words seemed to become richer in meaning. For a moment, Toren could feel all the Ru-Imbur's confusion and sadness. He knew that the Ru-Imbur loved the Pioneers, and yet he feared them, too. They solved problems by destroying. That was not the Imbur way. Commander Mallixxan seemed to understand, but he did not stop the killing.

The Ru-Imbur removed his hands, and the images in Toren's mind faded. Toren still sensed the problem, and it troubled him. He wanted so much to help. But he did not know how.

THE TWINING GRASS

Toren slept poorly that night. He kept waking up, thinking of the problems facing his father. Somehow, Commander Mallixxan had to find water. He had to figure out a way to bring it back to Pioneer Base One. And he had to prove to the Imbur that Earthmen were not really cruel, only frightened. How could he do all these things?

The next day, as they set out on the search, Toren told Rilmat of his worries. His friend felt sorry for him. Rilmat wanted to help, but could think of no solution.

The search teams travelled deep into the forest. They were now in a region totally unknown to the Pioneers. Few Imbur had ever travelled this far.

Here they found no trails or markings to guide them. And still no trace of water.

As they went on, they found the forest changing. The gampal trees were shrunken. The fruit was small and withered. It seemed that the lack of water was even worse here than elsewhere on the planet.

But not all the trees were dying. Some seemed healthy. Their fruit was a bright gold. Toren bit into one of the gampal fruits. It was juicy and delicious, just as it should have been.

Rilmat noticed the same thing. He and Toren studied the trees more closely. They sought some pattern to the healthy and unhealthy ones. When they found a row of very dry, very stunted gampal trees, they followed it to find some clue.

The undergrowth became thicker as they went on. At first it was only a bother. Soon, though, it made the walking difficult. A tangle of pale orange grass was everywhere on the ground. Some of the stalks were as thick as Toren's finger. As the searchers went on, the stalks became longer and higher. When they reached a point where the orange grass was knee-high, Toren stopped. He was hot, and tired, and very thirsty. The walking was very difficult. At every step, the orange grass clung to his boots.

Rilmat, too, was tired. They stopped under a gampal tree. Toren passed his canteen to Rilmat. They both needed a drink of cool water.

When Rilmat had drunk, Toren raised the canteen to his lips. As he started to drink, something tugged at his ankle. Rilmat cried out. The grass was moving all around them. It was closing in. Already, long strands were twined around Toren's legs. One of Rilmat's arms was encircled.

"What is this stuff, Rilmat?" Toren cried, tugging at the grass.

"I don't know. Help me, Toren!"

Toren tried to pull his feet free, but he could not. The orange grass was climbing higher all around him. One strand closed around his wrist, but he pulled it loose. Another encircled him, then another. He jerked one loose, but two others wrapped around his arm. He shouted as loud as he could, and Rilmat joined his cries. The orange grass kept pulling them down.

Toren felt a stinging in his arms and legs. It was like a lot of tiny needles pricking his skin. He shouted louder, and fought to stay on his feet.

"I can't stay up, Toren! It's pulling me down!" Rilmat cried.

"Try, Rilmat! Help will be here soon!"

"I can't! The tendrils are too strong for me!"

Toren tried to rip his feet free so he could help his friend. But he was anchored solidly. Tendrils of the orange grass were wound around his arms and legs. He felt himself being pulled to his knees. With all his remaining strength, he gave one last cry for help.

From far away came the voices of Earthmen. The sound gave Toren new hope. He struggled erect and called again and again. The voices of their rescuers came closer. Rilmat, too, found the strength to resist the pull of the orange strands for a little longer.

Commander Mallixxan burst from the forest. He headed straight for the two boys. As he ran, he drew his machete. With quick slashes, he freed Rilmat and then Toren. Toren was glad his father had saved Rilmat first.

Once Toren and Rilmat were out of danger, other Pioneers began to slash at the orange grass with their machetes. In a few moments, only stumps of the orange grass could be seen.

"Are you all right, son?" Commander Mallixxan asked.

Toren nodded. He did not want to talk yet. His voice felt shaky. Some tendrils still clung to his sleeve, and he pulled them off. Just touching them made him shiver.

"Let me have those tendrils, Toren," his father said. "We've never seen anything like this. I want to have it analyzed."

"It's awful stuff, Father," Toren said. "I felt it stinging me. It was like a lot of little needles."

"We'll have the doctor look at you and Rilmat right away," Commander Mallixxan said. He helped Toren to his feet. As they turned to leave, they faced the Ru-Imbur.

"You saved my son," the Imbur leader said. "I could not have come in time, or freed him from the growth."

"You saved Toren when he was lost in the forest and injured. I'm glad I could return the deed," Commander Mallixxan said.

The Ru-Imbur stepped back one pace, bowed, and raised his hands to his forehead. He repeated the gesture twice, then let them pass. Other Imbur made the same gesture as Toren and his father went by.

"What are they all doing? Isn't that their way of saying hello and good-bye?" Commander Mallixxan asked his son.

"When they repeat it like that, it's a sign of respect," Toren told him.

"Are you sure?"

"Yes. Rilmat told me so."

His father smiled and put his arm around Toren's shoulder. "It looks as though you helped me win back the Ru-Imbur. But next time, don't try so hard."

PIONEER
BASE
ONE

The Earthmen had a hospital and laboratory at Pioneer Base One. Commander Mallixxan brought Toren and Rilmat back on a supply skimmer. The Ru-Imbur remained in charge of the search teams.

Toren still had tiny red marks on his arms when they arrived. But he was not in pain. He felt as good as ever, except for a terrible thirst. Rilmat, too, was very thirsty. Commander Mallixxan gave them all the water he could spare, but it was not nearly enough.

As soon as they landed, the three went directly to the hospital. Doctor Wamukota, Chief Medical Officer of the base, was waiting for them. While

Toren and Rilmat were examined, Commander Mallixxan brought the samples of orange grass to the laboratory for analysis.

Doctor Wamukota placed Toren and Rilmat on tables at once. After a quick but thorough examination by machine, she examined them more closely. Her hands were very gentle as she felt the punctures in Toren's arm.

"Will we be all right, Doctor?" Toren asked.

"You appear to be in perfect health," she told him, smiling. "That orange grass didn't do anything but scare you."

"I'm awfully thirsty," Toren said.

"So am I," said Rilmat.

"Well, you can help yourselves to water, just this once," Doctor Wamukota told them.

Commander Mallixxan entered the examining room at this point, and heard the good news. He let out a sigh of relief.

"What about those red marks, Doctor?" he asked.

Wamukota shook her head. "I'm not sure about them, Commander. They seem to be fading very quickly and leaving no effect on the boys."

"Are you sure Toren and Rilmat haven't been poisoned in some way?" asked Commander Mallixxan.

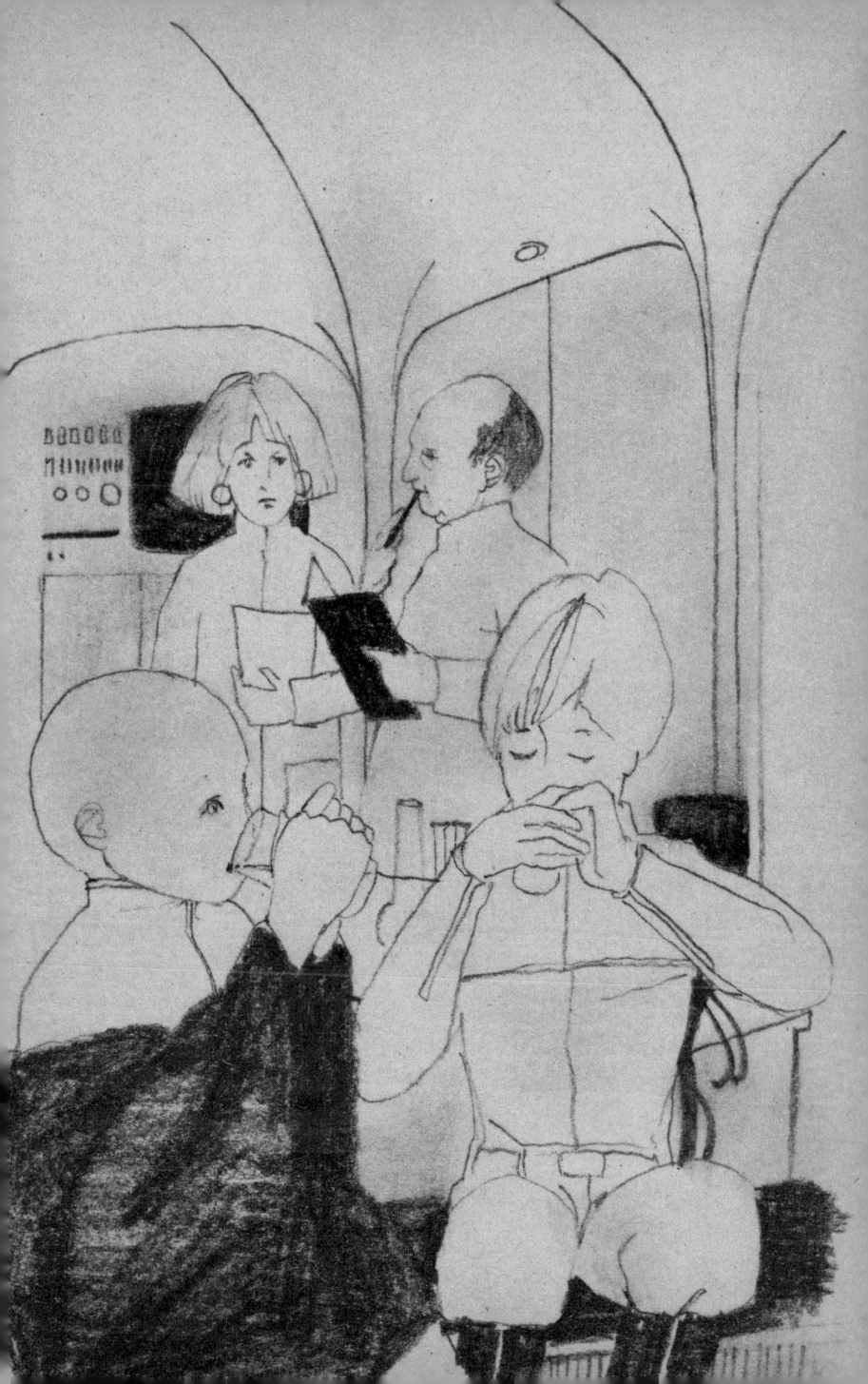

"Definitely not," the doctor said. "Nothing has been introduced into their bodies."

Commander Mallixxan was still concerned. "Has anything been taken out? Have they lost any blood?"

"No evidence of it," Doctor Wamukota said. "Their water level is low, but that's probably the result of working in the heat on short water rations."

"They were both very thirsty all the way back here."

When Commander Mallixxan said that, Doctor Wamukota looked very thoughtful, as if an idea had occurred to her. "Wait a minute, Commander — did the thirst begin after you rescued them?"

"Yes. I've never seen them so thirsty," Commander Mallixxan aid.

"They still are. They asked for water as soon as I finished the examination. Commander, I think we ought to go to the lab and see what they've learned about that plant."

"Do you think it may be poisonous after all?"

Doctor Wamukota shook her head. "Not poisonous. But it might be very dangerous."

THE SECRET OF THE ORANGE GRASS

The four of them went together to the base laboratory. Toren's mother met them at the entrance. She was in charge of the laboratory.

"Toren and Rilmat are fine," Commander Mallixxan assured her, even before she could ask. "What have you found out about the plant?"

She hugged the two boys and looked them over very closely for herself. When she saw the red marks on Toren's arms, she frowned.

"Don't worry, Mother," he said. "It doesn't hurt. I'm all right. Doctor Wamukota said so."

Taking the boys by the hand, Toren's mother led them into the lab. The others followed. Inside, she said to them, "This is a strange growth. It

seems to live only on water. And it can extract water from anything."

Commander Mallixxan looked puzzled. "If it lives on water, how can it be so healthy? This whole planet is drying up."

"I don't know. But look at this."

She cut a tiny piece of the orange grass. Placing it in a glass beaker, she filled the beaker with water. Before their eyes, with a speed that astonished them, the orange grass absorbed all the water. It began to grow in thin, threadlike strands.

"Maybe we're lucky there's a water shortage. That thing could cover the planet in a very short time," Commander Mallixxan said.

"There's another possibility," Toren's mother said. "The plant might be the cause of the shortage."

"That doesn't make sense," the Commander objected. "If this plant were draining off all the water, we'd see it before."

Rilmat had been silently studying the plant growing in the beaker. In a startled voice, he said, "This is the sorkampal. It *does* grow everywhere on our world!"

Commander Mallixxan said, "Why didn't you say so before, Rilmat?"

"I did not recognize it before. I have never seen

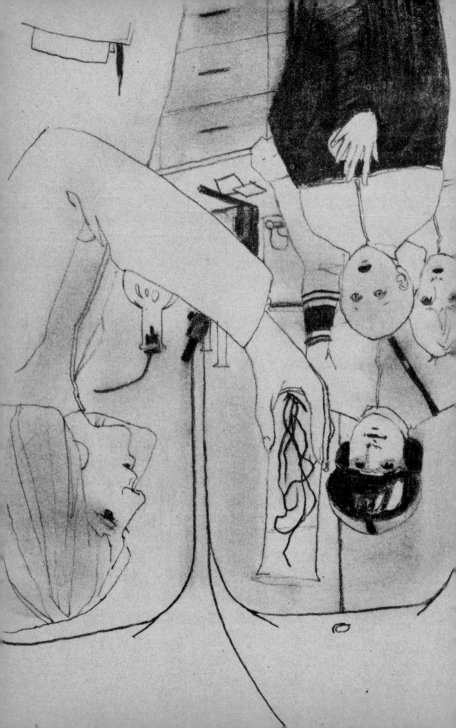

it growing so big. This is the size I know," he said, pointing to the threadlike strands in the beaker.

"Then that's the answer," Toren's mother said. "Something has made this plant grow, and now it's big enough to consume the water supply of the entire planet."

Doctor Wamukota said, "But what could have happened? Is it some kind of mutation?"

"No evidence of it," Toren's mother said. She turned to Rilmat. "What did you call the plant, Rilmat?"

"Sorkampal. In your language, that would mean food of the sork."

"Is this really what the sork eat?" Wamukota asked.

"Yes. They feed on the young shoots. So the sorkampal never grows larger than that piece," Rilmat said, pointing to the beaker. "That is why I did not recognize it at first."

"At least now we have an idea what's taking our water. Now, what can we do to reclaim it? Can we boil this stuff, or wring out the water?" Mallixxan asked.

His wife shook her head. "There's no way to reclaim the water. Somehow, this plant breaks water down completely. The only thing to do is control it. We must restore the old balance."

"We can't," Commander Mallixxan said. "We disturbed the old balance, but only the sork can restore it,"

"What do you mean, Father?" Toren asked.

"For ages, sork have fed on the orange grass. They ate the young shoots and kept it from growing large enough to disrupt the water supply. But then we came and started killing off the sork."

"So now there's nothing to control the sorkampal!" Toren cried.

Toren's mother looked at the plant in the beaker. "In a short time, that orange grass will cover all of Ziax II. Everything else will die out," she said.

Commander Mallixxan leaned his hands on the laboratory table and lowered his head. When he raised his eyes to look at his wife, Doctor Wamukota, and the two boys, his expression was very sad.

"Only the sork can save us," he said, "and we may have destroyed the last sork on Ziax II. If we have, then we've destroyed a whole planet, and ourselves with it."

THE
RU-IMBUR
SPEAKS

That night they slept at the base. Early next morning, Commander Mallixxan took Toren and Rilmat back to the forest.

It was a long ride. Looking from their skimmer, they could see great patches of withered gampal trees. In one place Rilmat pointed out a patch of sorkampal. It was almost as high as the trees and covered an area as large as Pioneer Base One. All around it the gampal trees were dead or dying.

Commander Mallixxan gazed down sadly. "It looks even worse from up here, doesn't it?" he said.

"Don't be discouraged, Commander," Rilmat said.

"At least we know what's causing the trouble," said Toren.

Commander Mallixxan nodded his head gravely. "We've caused the trouble. The Earthmen came to Ziax II and wiped out the sork. Without the sork, the orange grass grew out of control. Now it will destroy us all, and there's nothing we can do."

"The Ru-Imbur will find a way," Rilmat said.

"I hope so, Rilmat. It's beyond our power now," Commander Mallixxan admitted.

They travelled most of the day. Near dusk, they saw the base camp of the Ru-Imbur's search teams. Commander Mallixxan had sent word to all the others to join them here. Most of the Imbur and Pioneers were now assembled, awaiting the Pioneer Commander's arrival.

The Pioneer leaders and the Imbur Watchers met that night. Commander Mallixxan told the whole story to the group. When he was finished, those present began to offer their suggestions.

Some felt that the Pioneers and the Imbur should migrate to the far side of the planet. Others wanted to refit the spaceship that had brought the Pioneers to Ziax II from Earth. They hoped that the two races could find a new world together. But few people thought that these ideas would work.

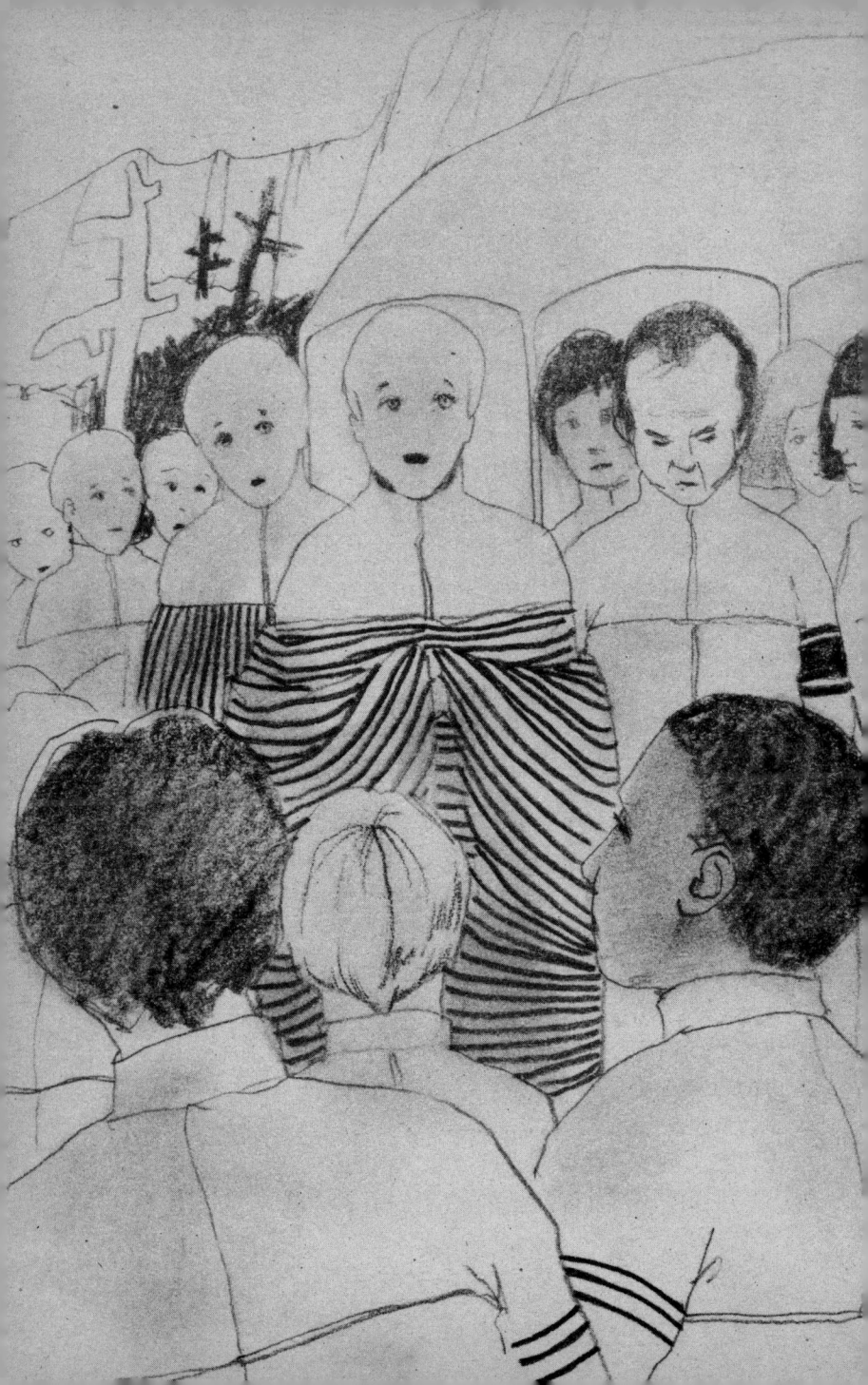

"Let's get together and find a way to destroy this sorkampal. That's our enemy," said one Pioneer.

Other Pioneers agreed with him. The Imbur were displeased. A Watcher rose to object.

"The sorkampal must not be destroyed," he said. "Its roots go deep, and help to hold the soil of our forest together."

Another Watcher said, "The sorkampal helps to draw water to the dry places of our planet. Destroy it, and the gampal forest will become a desert."

"It will become a desert a lot faster if we don't!" the Earthmen cried.

Commander Mallixxan raised his hands for order. Everyone was quiet. He spoke then, and his voice was low. He sounded very sad.

"Destroying the sorkampal or anything else won't help now," he said. "If we hadn't been so quick to destroy, we wouldn't be in trouble now. The Imbur warned us not to harm the sork. We didn't heed their warning. Now we find that the sork is necessary on this planet, just like the sorkampal. Living things are all related. They all depend on one another, in ways we don't always understand. No one has the right to destroy them. But we've learned our lesson too late. Because of the Pioneers, all on Ziax II are doomed."

"Perhaps not," said the Ru-Imbur.

Everyone turned to him. "What hope can there be?" a Pioneer asked.

"Perhaps the sork are not extinct. Perhaps they have only fled to a safer part of Ziax II," the Ru-Imbur replied.

"We've covered a lot of this planet in our search for water. Not one sork has been sighted," Commander Mallixxan said.

"There is one place we have not looked. No one has gone beyond the mountains," the Ru-Imbur said.

"They're sheer cliffs. The skimmers can't go there because the wind is too strong," one of the Pioneers said.

The Ru-Imbur looked at the Pioneer who had spoken. "And so the sork might have gone there, where his enemies cannot follow."

"That's a long chance to take," the Pioneer said.

"It will be very dangerous," said a Watcher.

Commander Mallixxan stepped to the side of the Ru-Imbur. His voice was no longer low and sad. Now he spoke like a leader.

"All of you are right," he said. "The sork may be beyond the mountains. It *is* a long way, and a long chance to take. It *will* be dangerous. But what choice do we have?"

One of the Pioneers objected. "We came out to

hunt water, sir. We're not prepared."

"I'll send the skimmers back for everything we need. Now we're going to hunt sork. This time, we want to save them."

THE
HUNT

The skimmers were sent back to Pioneer Base One that very night. By late the next day, they began to return. Every skimmer that could fly was ordered to the assembly point. They came loaded down with food and equipment for the Pioneers and the Imbur.

Days of planning and long meetings followed. Everyone was busy. At last the preparations were complete. Early one morning, a great fleet of skimmers lifted from the clearing deep in the forest. In close formation they headed for the polar mountain range. No one had ever crossed that range before. Now if they were to save their planet, the Pioneers and the Imbur had to go

where they had never dared to go before.

The skimmers travelled at top speed. For two full days the gampal forest sped by beneath them. Toren and Rilmat stayed by the side of their skimmer, looking at everything below. They saw what appeared to be a stream bed and a small pond. Both were dry and filled with the orange grass. Commander Mallixxan saw these things, too, and he turned away and said nothing. But he was not an Imbur. Toren could read his expression. He could tell that his father was worried. The water that might have saved them was not being found.

Late on the second day of travel they passed the last of the gampal trees. These were small and stunted and very wide apart. Now the ground was bare beneath them, except for large patches of the orange grass.

They saw the peaks of the mountain range rising far away. Another full day of travel brought them to the foothills. By this time, the winds were getting strong. The skimmers were difficult to control.

Commander Mallixxan ordered them to fly lower. The formation spread out for greater safety. They flew so close to the ground that Toren felt as if he could reach down and touch it.

Still the winds grew stronger. When two skimmers nearly collided, Commander Mallixxan ordered all to land. From this point, they would travel on foot.

They set up their base camp where they landed. Commander Mallixxan had brought enough tents for everyone. Even though they did not like to sleep enclosed in a tent, the Imbur were satisfied to use them now, in this part of Ziax II. The wind was cold and penetrating. There were no gampal trees here to provide vines for weaving shelter. No one knew what kind of creatures might come upon them during the night. A tent was shelter and protection.

Scouting parties went out the next day. Toren and Rilmat were ordered to stay at the base camp. They were unhappy, but they did not argue. The scouts would be out only for a little while, then they would come back to report. The important thing was to go with the main search team.

After they had eaten, Toren and Rilmat went to the edge of the camp and looked at the landscape. The sheer rock rose before them like a wall. There seemed to be no way to climb over those cliffs, and no way to get through. If this were so, could any sork have made it past them? Toren wondered. Perhaps they had come all this way for nothing.

One by one the scouting parties returned. All had bad news. The mountain face was sheer, they said. No pass could be found. Some thought that a skimmer might make it to the top, but it would be blown out of control before it could land.

And then one scouting party returned with good news. They had found a pass to the other side. At the entrance to the pass, they saw traces of sork.

When they heard this news, the Pioneers and the Imbur began to shout for joy. Toren and Rilmat joined in the shouts. Suddenly Toren began to laugh. The sork had long been their worst enemy on the planet, and now they were cheering to learn it still survived! But the sork, they had learned, was an enemy no longer. It was part of the life of Ziax II. It was necessary. It was a friend.

THE
RESCUE

The leaders went through the pass first. Other Pioneers and Imbur followed them. Toren and Rilmat were almost the last ones to go through.

When they finally came to the far opening, the sight of the others was a surprise. Everyone looked very serious and sad. Toren heard them speak of their disappointment. He looked over the ridge before him, and down into the valley beyond. The sorkampal was everywhere. He saw no ice or snow, even though it was cold here. The sorkampal had absorbed all the moisture from the air.

Toren went to his father. Commander Mallix-xan put his arm around his son's shoulder, but said nothing.

"Does this mean the sork are all gone?" Toren asked.

Commander Mallixxan nodded his head. He looked around at his men and the Imbur and the two boys. "The sork is extinct," he said. "Soon the sorkampal will cover all of Ziax II. We can't control it and we can't destroy it. We have no way to reclaim the water it absorbs. We've destroyed a world and its people."

The Ru-Imbur stepped to his side. "You must not say that. As long as we live, we can hope. Let us..."

A loud roar shook the ground, drowning out the Ru-Imbur's words. Another roar followed, even louder. Then came the sounds of struggle, of loud crashing and ripping of sorkampal.

"A sork!" Commander Mallixxan cried.

"Many sork!" shouted the Ru-Imbur.

The leaders gave orders. Earthmen and Imbur quickly moved into formation and started cutting a path toward the sounds. The noise grew louder and more frightening as they came closer. It sounded as though an army of sork were in a great battle.

The searchers came upon six of the creatures. Two sork were full-grown, and the others were small. They were surrounded by sorkampal stalks

taller than the tallest gampal trees. The stalks were closing in on the beasts, as they had done to Toren and Rilmat. The sork were tearing at the stalks with their great claws and teeth. But the sork were slowly overpowered. One small sork, about the size of a calf, had been pulled to the ground. It was squealing in pain and fright. The adult sork were trying to reach it, but they, too, were entangled in the thick stalks. The sorkampal was too strong for them.

The Earthmen moved forward in a line, slashing at the sorkampal with their machetes. The Imbur stayed close behind them. Working furiously, the Pioneers cleared a path to the sork's side, then stopped.

The sork turned their attention to the humans. As long as the orange stalks held them pinned, they could do no harm. But they had to be freed. Commander Mallixxan looked to his men, then to the Ru-Imbur. The leader of the Imbur signaled his readiness.

At Commander Mallixxan's order, the entire party of Pioneers moved ahead at once. They cut away the last strands of sorkampal. Once the sork were free, the Earthmen quickly fell back. Now the Imbur moved forward.

At first, the sork were stunned. Then they

turned to attack the intruders. But the Imbur had already begun their sork chant. The huge beasts roared a warning, then rushed at the chanting Imbur. The Imbur stood their ground. The sork staggered, roared weakly, and stumbled. Then they fell and lay still, in a deep sleep.

WORKING
TOGETHER

The hardest part of the whole journey was carrying the sork back to camp. After that, each sork was placed on a skimmer to be brought back to Pioneer Base One as soon as possible.

Toren and Rilmat rode with Commander Mallixxan in a small, fast skimmer. They carried with them one of the baby sork. Toren felt just a little bit uneasy about their passenger. True, the sork was smaller than he was. And it was sleeping peacefully. But it had teeth and claws and big slitted eyes, just like a full-grown adult. And big or small, it was a *sork*. Rilmat acted uneasy, too.

Commander Mallixxan noticed the two of them sitting on the opposite side of the skimmer from the sork. He went over and sat down beside them.

"Is everything all right?" he asked.

"Oh, yes. Everything is fine," they said.

"You aren't worried about anything, are you?"

"Well...the sork..." Toren said uncomfortably.

"That little fellow? He won't give us any trouble. If he moves, you can quiet him down with the chant," Commander Mallixxan said.

Toren and Rilmat looked at each other. They trusted the sork chant, but still, a skimmer is a very small place to share with a sork. Even a very small, sleepy sork.

"I'm surprised at the two of you," Commander Mallixxan said, smiling good-naturedly at them. "We know the sork chant works. All the Pioneers are willing to trust it now. We had to depend on it back there and it worked perfectly."

"That was awfully close," Toren said, remembering the rescue.

"It was. The timing had to be perfect. It was risky, but it had to be done that way," his father said.

Rilmat asked, "Why didn't we put the sork to sleep first, so the Pioneers would be safe?"

"We couldn't, Rilmat. The sork had to be awake and fighting until the very last minute. It was the only way we could save them all."

Toren nodded. "And every one of them counts, now."

"They certainly do," his father agreed. "We'll release them as soon as we land. In a very short time, they'll have the sorkampal under control."

"Is there a chance that we might have to rescue them again?" Rilmat asked.

"Yes. That's a real danger," said the Commander. "We'll have to keep a guard on them until we're sure they're safe. The Ru-Imbur and I will see to that. We'll have to work closely from now on."

"It seems funny," Toren said. "First we nearly wipe the sork out, and then we turn around and risk our lives to save it and protect it."

"We've been very lucky. We learned something important about our planet. And it's time we learned something else, too."

"What else?" Toren and Rilmat asked.

"The sork chant," Commander Mallixxan said. "We'll never use a weapon against the sork again. But until they become tame — and that might be a long time — we have to protect ourselves. The Ru-Imbur and I have talked it over, and we feel that you two would be the best ones to teach us. How about it?"

"We can do it," Rilmat said.

"In fact," Toren said, looking at the sleeping sork, "as soon as that fellow starts to move, we'll begin the first lesson!"